P9-DCO-242

MOLLY AND THE MOVIE STAR

MOLLY · 1944

BY VALERIE TRIPP

ILLUSTRATIONS NICK BACKES

VIGNETTES SUSAN MCALILEY

THE AMERICAN GIRLS COLLECTION®

Published by Pleasant Company Publications
Previously published in *American Girl*® magazine
© Copyright 2000 by Pleasant Company
For information, address: Book Editor, Pleasant Company Publications,
8400 Fairway Place, P.O. Box 620998, Middleton, WI 53562.

Printed in Singapore.
00 01 02 03 04 05 06 07 TWP 10 9 8 7 6 5 4 3 2 1

Edited by Camela Decaire, Nancy Holyoke, and Michelle Jones
Designed by Laura Moberly and Kimberly Strother
Art Directed by Katie Brown, Myland McRevey,
Julie Mierkiewicz, and Kimberly Strother

Library of Congress Cataloging-in-Publication Data

Tripp, Valerie, 1951-
Molly and the movie star / by Valerie Tripp ; illustrations,
Nick Backes ; vignettes, Susan McAliley.
p. cm. — (The American girls collection)
Summary: Molly is eager to meet a famous movie star at a
War Bond rally, until she cannot find the money that her class had
collected to buy a bond. Includes information on movies during
World War II and a recipe for popcorn.

ISBN 1-58485-036-1
1. World War, 1939-1945—United States Juvenile fiction.
[1. World War, 1939-1945—United States Fiction.
2. Actors and actresses Fiction. 3. Schools Fiction.]
I. Backes, Nick, ill. II. Title. III. Series.
PZ7.T7363Mm 2000   [Fic]—dc21   99-40580 CIP

TABLE OF CONTENTS

MOLLY'S FAMILY

DAD
*Molly's father, a doctor
who is somewhere in
England, taking care of
wounded soldiers.*

MOM
*Molly's mother, who
holds the family together
while Dad is away.*

MOLLY
*A nine-year-old who
is growing up on
the home front
in America during
World War Two.*

JILL
*Molly's fourteen-year-old
sister, who is always trying
to act grown-up.*

RICKY
*Molly's twelve-year-old
brother—a big pest.*

BRAD
*Molly's five-year-old
brother—a little pest.*

LINDA
*One of Molly's best friends,
a practical schemer.*

SUSAN
*Molly's other best friend,
a cheerful dreamer.*

MRS. GILFORD
*The housekeeper,
who rules the roost when
Mom is at work.*

MOLLY AND THE MOVIE STAR

Molly McIntire burst into the kitchen running so fast her brown braids stuck straight out behind her. "Guess what!" she exclaimed. "My class is collecting money to buy a War Bond at the big rally a week from Saturday, and *I'm* going to give the money to Melody Moore! Can you believe it?"

"My goodness!" said Mom.

Mrs. Gilford, the housekeeper, asked, "Who's Melody Moore?"

1

Molly gasped. "You mean you don't know?" she said. "Melody Moore is a *very* famous movie star. She's coming to *our* town. Everybody will come to the rally to see her, and she'll sing and dance and make everybody feel patriotic and happy so they'll buy War Bonds."

"Well," Mrs. Gilford began, "War Bonds are a good thing, but—"

"Oh, I know!" interrupted Molly proudly. "That's how I was chosen to give our money to Melody Moore. I explained War Bonds the best of anyone in my class. I said you buy a War Bond for eighteen dollars and seventy-five cents. The government uses the money to buy things for our soldiers. But the government is really only borrowing the money, because in ten years you can take your War Bond to a bank and get twenty-five dollars for it."

"Very good!" said Mom.

"As I was saying," Mrs. Gilford went on firmly, "War Bonds are good. But I don't see why the rallies have to be flim-flam shows, with glamour girls singing and all. People should buy the bonds to help our fighting boys because it's the right thing to do."

"Yes! Well!" said Mom. "How much money are you supposed to bring in, Molly?"

"About a dollar, I guess," said Molly.

"I have fifty cents in my bank I can use."

"And you can use your movie money for tomorrow and next Saturday," added Mom.

"Oh, no," said Molly. "I *have* to go to the movie tomorrow. Melody Moore is in it. I'll *earn* the money I need for the War Bond. I'll put on a show, or paint the garage, or—"

"You can do chores," said Mrs. Gilford. "If you mop the kitchen floor, sort the laundry, polish the silver, and rake the Victory garden, I'd say that would be worth fifty cents."

Molly frowned. Chores were dull. She wanted to do something

4

exciting to earn the money.

But Mom was already saying, "Molly, I'll give you the money Friday if Mrs. Gilford says you've done the chores to her satisfaction."

"Okay," Molly sighed. *Anyway, the chores will be easy*, she thought.

The next day, when Molly went to the movies with her best friends Linda and Susan, she was very glad she had not given up her movie money. Molly loved everything about going to the movies. She and Linda and Susan liked to get to the theater early, buy their tickets, and then walk slowly around the lobby, studying the posters of coming attractions. They liked to have plenty of time to gaze at the candy in the big glass case. Molly always ended up getting popcorn, but Linda and Susan tried something new each week—candy bars or licorice twists, caramels or taffy. The girls said hi to all their friends from school as they arrived. Almost everyone came to the movies on Saturday afternoon.

This afternoon, Molly settled into her seat as the theater went dark. The curtains parted. The music swelled. As the movie began, Molly shivered with pleasure. There was Melody Moore on the screen, larger than life,

wearing a Red Cross nurse's uniform!
Oh, thought Molly, *I can't wait till I meet
Melody Moore.*

After the movie, the girls walked
to the McIntires' house. "Well, girls. How
was the movie?" Mrs. Gilford asked.

"Melody Moore was great," Molly
said. "She was so brave when she was

taking care of the soldiers in the field hospital."

"I loved it when she and the other nurses sang and danced for the soldiers," said Linda.

All three girls sang the song from the movie: "I'm a soldier in the army of lo-ove . . ."

Mrs. Gilford muttered, "Nurses singing and dancing. Nonsense!"

Susan said, "There's one thing I don't get. Why didn't Melody Moore tell that tall soldier before he left that she loved him? Why did she hide a letter in his sock in his duffel bag?"

"Because!" exclaimed Molly. "You can't go around blabbing

to someone that you love him! Hiding the letter in his sock was much more romantic."

"Oh," said Susan. "But that other nurse, the one with fingernail polish, kissed him before he left. I was afraid he was going to fall in love with her instead of Melody Moore."

"Of course not," said Molly. "He loved Melody Moore from the first moment he saw her. He fell in love with her when she did that special salute." Molly tilted her head, winked, saluted, and twirled on her toes.

"Gosh, Molly," said Linda. "You do that salute exactly like Melody Moore!"

"Yes," sighed Susan. "Molly, you are

so lucky. I just can't believe you're really, truly going to meet Melody Moore at the rally."

"The point of the rally is to buy War Bonds, *not* to ogle movie stars," said Mrs. Gilford. "Molly hasn't even begun to earn the money she's supposed to give to the War Bond fund."

Molly said quickly, "I'll do the chores, Mrs. Gilford. I'll start tomorrow."

But the next day, Sunday, Susan invited Molly and Linda over to listen to Melody Moore records. So Molly didn't begin her chores until Monday after school. She got off to a bad start. She tried to rake the leaves out of the Victory garden, but the wind kept blowing them back in.

When Mrs. Gilford came to check on her work, Molly said crossly, "I shouldn't be working outside in this weather. What if I catch a cold? I don't want Melody Moore to see me with a red nose."

"Rake harder," said Mrs. Gilford. "That'll warm you up."

As the days passed, the indoor chores didn't go much better. Mrs. Gilford made Molly polish the silver twice, because it was streaky the first time. Molly had to mop the kitchen floor twice, too, because she forgot to rinse it the first time. *I bet Melody Moore never does house-work*, thought Molly. She held the mop as if it were a microphone and looked at her reflection in the toaster. "I'm a soldier in the army of lo-ove," she sang.

Molly stopped. Mrs. Gilford was standing in the doorway watching her. "Molly," she said sternly, "the trouble with you is that you are so caught up with your imaginary movie friends, you can't keep your mind on the task before you."

The trouble with Mrs. Gilford is that she has no imagination, Molly thought later. *She only cares about boring things like scrubbing floors. Mrs. Gilford could never be like a heroine in a movie. She could never do anything brave or dramatic. Never.*

On Friday morning, Mom asked, "How did Molly do with the chores,

Mrs. Gilford?" Molly stood still. She was not sure what Mrs. Gilford would say.

"Well," said Mrs. Gilford, "she hasn't sorted the laundry yet."

Mom turned to Molly. "You'll sort the laundry after school, won't you, Molly?"

"Yes," answered Molly.

"Then here's the money you earned," said Mom, handing two quarters to Molly.

"Thanks, Mom," said Molly. She hurried off to school to add her dollar to the War Bond fund. Her teacher, Miss Campbell, replaced all the change with dollar bills. She put the bills in an envelope and handed it to Molly.

"We're trusting you to take care of

this money, Molly," said Miss Campbell. "We're proud that you'll represent us at the War Bond rally."

Molly put the envelope in her book-bag and buckled it securely. She held the bookbag with both hands as she walked to Susan's house after school. She kept the bag next to her while she and Linda and Susan listened to Melody Moore records. She held it tight as she ran home, just in time for dinner.

Mrs. Gilford met her with a grim look. "You forgot about sorting the laundry."

"Oh!" said Molly. "Whoops! I'm sorry."

"I hope so," said Mrs. Gilford. "I'm

going now. Your sister Jill is in charge until your mother gets home, which will be very late. After dinner, I want you to sort the laundry. Put everything that needs to be mended in the basket. Your mother can drop the mending off at my house tomorrow morning on the way to the rally. She has to go early. I have no wish to go to that circus of a rally myself." Mrs. Gilford tied her scarf under her chin in a tight knot. "It'll do you good to have a task tonight. It'll keep your mind off this Melanie Moon nonsense."

"Melody Moore," said Molly.

"Whatever," said Mrs. Gilford. Then she left.

After dinner, Molly's sister Jill and her brothers Ricky and Brad went into the living room to listen to a radio program. Molly felt rather forlorn in the kitchen all by herself, sorting the clean laundry into piles. Almost all of Ricky's socks went into the mending pile to be darned. Molly wiggled her finger through a hole in the heel of one sock. *It's a good thing the sock Melody Moore hid her love note in didn't have a hole like this,* she thought.

Suddenly, Molly had an inspiration. She could put the War Bond money in a sock and hand the sock to Melody Moore at the rally tomorrow! That way Melody

Moore would know she had seen her movie. And Molly could do her special tilt, wink, salute, and twirl, too. Melody Moore would love it! She would say, "Molly McIntire, you're a star!" Putting the money in a sock was a great idea!

Quickly, Molly ran upstairs with one of Ricky's socks that didn't have a hole. She took the envelope with the money, folded it, and put it in the toe of the sock. It was perfect! It was just like in the movie! Molly stood in front of her mirror and practiced handing the sock to Melody Moore and saluting her special salute over and over. Tilt, wink, salute, twirl. Tilt, wink, salute, twirl. Finally, she put the sock on her chair with her

Putting the money in a sock was a great idea!

clothes, so she would not forget it the next morning. She went to bed humming, "I'm a soldier in the army of lo-ove!"

Molly was too nervous to sleep well. She was half awake when her mother came in to kiss her goodnight. By the time Molly woke up the next morning, Mom had already left the house.

This is it! thought Molly. *This is the day I meet a movie star!* She jumped out of bed. When she looked at her chair, she froze in horror. The sock! The sock with the money was gone! Frantically, Molly threw everything off the chair. She looked under the chair, under the bed, in the closet, then under the chair again. Nothing.

She ran down the hall into Ricky's room and began tossing socks out of his drawer. "Ricky, wake up!" she shouted. "Did you take one of your socks out of my room last night?"

"No," said Ricky. "What's—" But Molly was already gone.

She flew down the stairs to the kitchen. Jill was sitting at the table, calmly drinking juice. "Jill!" gasped Molly. "Did you take one of Ricky's socks out of my room last night?"

"No," said Jill.

"Where could it be?" wailed Molly. "I hid the money for my class's War Bond in the sock, and now it's gone!"

"What?" exclaimed Jill. "Why did

you put the money in a sock?"

"I wanted it to be like in Melody Moore's movie," said Molly.

Jill sighed. "You and your big ideas," she said. "Well, let's search the house. The sock has to be here somewhere."

Molly and Jill started searching and did not stop until they'd looked in every nook and cranny of the house. Even Ricky and Brad helped them search. Finally, they gave up. The sock was nowhere to be found.

"What am I going to do?" moaned Molly.

"You'll have to go to the rally and explain what happened," said Ricky.

"I can't!" said Molly. "I'd rather

die than tell Melody Moore what I did!"

"Write her a confession note," Jill said.

"Yeah," said Ricky. "Hide it in a sock."

"No!" said Molly and Jill together.

"But what'll I tell my class?" Molly asked. "They'll all hate me."

"Tell them you'll pay the money back," said Ricky. "If you don't go to the movies for two hundred weeks, which is about four years, you'll have twenty dollars. Then you can pay back the money you lost."

"Well," sighed Molly. "After this, I don't think I'll ever want to go to the movies again for the rest of my life."

As soon as Molly's note was ready, she and Jill and Brad and Ricky left for the rally. Molly felt as if she were marching to her execution as they walked to the high school football field.

Molly took her seat on the stage that was set up at one end of the field, and looked out at the crowd. She felt hot with shame and cold with fear. She slid her confession note out of her pocket and reread it. *Miss Moore,* it said. *Please don't read this out loud. I lost my class's money. I will pay it back. I am sorry. Your fan, Molly McIntire.*

Just then, the crowd started to murmur. An army jeep stopped at the edge of the field. Molly held her breath as the crowd started to cheer. Because there she was! There was Melody Moore, smiling and waving and walking through the crowd. She looked as beautiful as she did in the movies!

Melody Moore danced up the steps of the stage and flashed a huge smile. The crowd whistled and clapped and yelled. The band played "I'm a soldier in the army of lo-ove," and everyone sang along with Melody Moore. Everyone, that is, except Molly. She was too miserable.

Then Melody Moore held her hands up for quiet. "I'm so pleased to be here," she said. "I know everyone in town wants to buy a War Bond today, especially the children of Willow Street School. Let's give these kids a hand!"

The crowd clapped and shouted. The band played a drumroll as a cute kindergartner handed an envelope to Melody Moore. The drummer hit the cymbals, and the crowd whooped and whistled when Melody Moore kissed the little first-grader who handed her an envelope. Everyone laughed and cheered for the second-grader who shook Melody Moore's hand too long. Molly could hardly breathe. Her turn was next! She stood up to walk across the stage toward Melody Moore. The drums began to roll.

The crowd quieted. *If only the world would end now,* Molly thought.

HONK! blasted the horn of the jeep. Molly just about jumped out of her skin. Everyone looked over at the jeep. HONK! HONK! The jeep nosed its way through the crowd, honking wildly. People jostled one another to clear a path. Molly looked and gasped. She could not believe her eyes. It was Mrs. Gilford!

Mrs. Gilford? thought Molly. *What on earth is she doing here?* Mrs. Gilford looked like the fearless general of an invading army. She was standing up in the jeep next to the driver. With one hand she held on to the windshield, and with the other hand she waved something over her head.

"Miss Moon!" Mrs. Gilford called out dramatically. "Stop immediately!"

The jeep pulled up next to the stage, and Mrs. Gilford climbed out. She strode up the steps with determination, nodded briskly to Melody Moore, and said, "Just a moment, Miss Moon." Then she walked straight over to Molly and handed her Ricky's sock. "Your mother picked up this sock by mistake and brought it to my house with the mending," Mrs. Gilford said. "I knew how important it was as soon as I saw it."

Molly was flooded with joy and relief. "Oh, Mrs. Gilford, thank you!" she whispered.

Mrs. Gilford looked like the fearless general of an invading army.

Mrs. Gilford smiled at Molly and gave her a nudge toward Melody Moore. "Go along, now," she said. "Your movie star is waiting."

Molly flew across the stage and handed Melody Moore the sock.

Melody Moore laughed. She pulled the envelope out of the sock, opened it, and waved the money at the crowd. She smiled at Molly.

"I can see that you're a real fan!" she said. "What's your name, sweetheart?"

"Molly McIntire," said Molly.

"Well, thank you, Molly," said Melody Moore. "And thank your grandmother, too."

"Oh, she's not my grandmother,"

said Molly. "That's Mrs. Gilford. She's my . . . she's my friend." *Good old Mrs. Gilford,* Molly thought. *She came to my rescue, just like a heroine in a movie.* Molly smiled at Mrs. Gilford, then turned to Melody Moore. Molly tilted her head, winked, saluted, and twirled on her toes. Melody Moore did the same thing right back, and the audience exploded into applause.

"Molly McIntire," said Melody Moore, "you're a star!"

VALERIE TRIPP

At 9   Now

When I was little, my sisters and I loved to go to the movies on rainy Saturday afternoons. I can imagine how excited Molly must have been about meeting a movie star. It was a dream come true. It would have been for me back then, I'm sure.

Valerie Tripp has written twenty-nine books in The American Girls Collection, including eight about Molly.

LOOKING
BACK
1944

A Peek Into
the Past

MOVIES IN 1944

Times were tough for girls growing up during World War Two. They had to do without a lot of things they wanted or needed. Many girls had fathers and brothers fighting overseas. The world was a pretty scary place.

But on Saturdays everything seemed different. Saturday was movie day—the best day of the week. For ten cents each, girls and boys in town could spend the afternoon at the theater. Saturday matinees showed double features!

Walking into the theater lobby was like entering another world. Many theaters were like palaces, with sparkling chandeliers and plush carpeting. Uniformed ushers took tickets. It was grand and exciting.

Even better, the lobbies smelled of lemon drops, Milk Duds, peppermints, and hot popcorn—treats hard to get during wartime. The candy and popcorn cost just five cents.

Gene Autry and his horse, Champion, were in many Westerns.

And that was just the start. Before the double feature, there might be singers and dancers performing in front of the screen. There might be a contest on stage, with free toys as prizes. You could count on seeing a cartoon or a short Western, with plenty of horses and cowboys. You might also get to see an episode in a *serial*, which left you hanging until the next week, when another episode would be shown.

You were allowed to cheer or boo during the show, and even walk around the theater, talking to your friends. Sometimes, though, the feature movie was so glamorous or so sad that no one thought to talk. One week it might be an adventure movie, like *Lassie Come Home*, in which a courageous dog travels miles to be with his master. Another week it

Lassie®

might be a scary science fiction movie about an earth invasion from outer space.

During wartime, many movies were about being in the military. Brave, glamorous soldiers and pilots fought exciting battles against German and Japanese "bad guys." There were

Since You Went Away—
a home-front movie

"home-front movies" too, which showed families just like Molly's learning how to live without brothers and fathers and uncles.

In the intermission between films, theaters showed black-and-white *newsreels,* which reported on the progress of the war. The newsreels showed actual land, air, and sea battles. The mood in the theater would change during the newsreels. Some people would begin to cry. Others shouted at the images of German and Japanese soldiers. And some people were scared. "I felt I was actually there," remembered one girl. Another girl always timed a trip to the bathroom so she would miss seeing the newsreels completely!

At the end of the day, girls went

Newsreel

home to read magazines like *Modern Screen*, which were all about their favorite movie stars. They could even join fan clubs. If they were lucky, a movie star might visit their hometown. During the war many movie stars traveled the country, joining rallies to sell War Bonds, singing in variety shows to help boost people's spirits, and pitching in however they could to help the war effort.

Movie star Shirley Temple in **Modern Screen**

Movie stars took their roles in the war very seriously. They knew that movies could offer an escape from the troubles of war. But they could also provide encouragement for people on the home front, and even inspire them to join the army or to take war jobs. Most of all, movies helped remind everyone that no matter the hardships, the war was worth fighting.

Movie star Joan Crawford at a War Bond rally

AN AMERICAN GIRLS PASTIME

An Afternoon
at the Movies
Set up a Saturday matinee!

As soon as the lights went down
in the theater, Molly was spellbound.
Each week, she was sure there couldn't
be a better movie than the one she'd
just watched.

Invite some friends, pop some
popcorn, and watch a movie that Molly
would have seen in 1944. You'll be spellbound, too!

MOVIE

Rent one of these movies, or

Lassie Come Home This movie was first shown in 1943. It was so popular that books, comics, and even a TV series about Lassie were made after it!

Since You Went Away Shirley Temple plays a girl a lot like Molly. Her father is away at war, and she and her mother and sister have to make a lot of changes.

PICKS

...orrow one from your library.

National Velvet Twelve-year-old Velvet
Brown loves horses. When she finally gets
a horse of her own, she sets her sights on
the greatest horse race in England.

Cinderella This classic fairy tale is as
popular now as it was when Molly first
saw it.

YOU WILL NEED:

An adult to help you

Medium saucepan with a lid

2 tablespoons vegetable oil

½ cup popping corn

Large bowl

Salt

Molly couldn't add butter or other toppings to her popcorn because of war shortages. But you can spice up your popcorn with one of these fun flavorings.

- melted butter
- cinnamon and sugar
- garlic salt and butter
- Parmesan cheese
- spicy Cajun seasoning

1. Pour the oil into the pan. Place the pan on a burner, and set the heat on medium-high.

2. Put 2 kernels of popcorn into the pan. When they pop, pour in the rest of the kernels and cover the pan with the lid.

3. When the kernels start popping, turn the heat down to low. Shake the pan back and forth so that the kernels don't burn. When the popping slows down, turn off the burner.

4. Pour the popped popcorn into a bowl, and add salt.